Short Stories

for

Busy People

by

Dr Leon Bernstein

First published 2008 by Lulu.com

Text ©2008 Dr Leon Bernstein
Cover Illustration copyright

This book has been typeset in Garamond

All rights reserved. No part of this book may be reproduced, transmitted or stored in an information retrieval system in any form or by any means, graphics, electronic or mechanical, including photocopying, taping or recording, without prior written permission of the copyright owner.

ISBN 978-1-4092-8484-0

Readers may contact the author on drleonbernstein@gmail.com

Acknowledgements

This anthology of short stories was inspired by my family and friends, whilst discussing one day the joy of living and making use of every moment we have. Since my mind is always buzzing with ideas and stories, it was suggested I write them down and share them with others.

I am grateful, as ever, to my wonderful wife Janice, who allows me the freedom of mind and spirit to be so creative, and to my equally wonderful children, Simon, Aaron, Devorah and Chana Tzivia, for their encouragement and their positive criticism on each story.

To Sharon Brand I owe a debt of thanks. Her perception, sensitivity and attention to detail in proof-reading the texts have been both beneficial and inspiring.

Finally, I am fortunate to be surrounded constantly by so many wonderful people, and have been privileged to have made such good friends during my stay in Australia. To them, and to you, the reader, I thank you.

Dr Leon Bernstein
Sydney, Australia
October 2008

Contents

Mr Tanner	7
Sarah's Doll	29
David, the Karate Kid	35
The Bee	45
The Elevator	51
The Fiddler	61
Route 49	67
The Grudge	77
Image	99
Billet-Doux	105

Mr Tanner

When his alarm sounded, Mr Tanner woke up with a start, slapped the 'off' button on top of the clock then sat up in bed, blinking twice. It was still dark, and he softly slipped out of bed, aware of his wife still sleeping peacefully in the stillness of their little room in the semi-detached house at the corner of Niblik Street, Eastern Suburbs of Sydney, Australia. As he left the bedroom, he was oblivious to the creaky floorboard which groaned under his weight, and which was responsible for waking his wife. Looking at the digits on her luminous watch, she slowly shook her head, sighed, then put on her slippers to join her husband who had crept downstairs towards the kitchen.

Mr Tanner, a man in his forties, could not be described as anything other than 'ordinary'. He had an ordinary job, wore ordinary clothes (apart from his outdated, thick-rimmed black glasses which he refused to part with) and lived what could only be described as an ordinary life. But he was about to begin a day which would later be viewed as truly extraordinary, even though nobody in the world but he (and later his wife) would know of it. In fact, prior to this day, Mr Tanner could not really think of anything at all that had been 'extraordinary' in his life. He had gone to the local school and had achieved the usual expected results. He had made many acquaintances and a few good friends before starting a university degree, which he finished in the normal time span, then began work as a local accountant before meeting, and subsequently marrying, his devoted wife. Their two married children lived nearby and frequently came to visit, and although Jeremy and Millie would bring their "loud, tiresome and moulting dog," as Mrs Tanner would often complain, there was always a harmonious family atmosphere whenever they were all together.

Mrs Tanner was therefore concerned that her husband's appointment with the optometrist, or "eye doctor" as he insisted on calling him, seemed to be causing him anxiety and was upsetting the children, who had noticed a recent unease in their father's demeanour. When she reached the bottom of the stairs she peered into the living room and saw him sitting in a chair facing the back garden. His dressing gown had been neatly folded on the sofa and the vapour from the hot mug of tea in his cupped hands was causing his glasses to mist up.

"Don't worry, dear, it'll be just fine," she said in a comforting and loving voice, folding down the upturned collar of his pyjamas. Mr Tanner turned his gaze away from the pitch black garden and looked at his wife.

"I'm not worried," he replied gently.

"Then what are you doing up at four o'clock in the morning?" she asked with a slight tone of despair.

"I'm up because I set my alarm to wake me up," he said with an air of mild assertion. "You see," he began, "I want to make the most use of my time before the operation tomorrow. You never know what might happen."

"But darling," she continued sympathetically, "they say millions of people have this treatment every day and there's a ninety-nine percent chance of a complete success!"

Mr Tanner looked intently at his wife, tried to smile but couldn't, then explained, "*They*, whoever *they* are, say lots of things my dear. But they are not having their eyes operated on tomorrow, I am! And what if *they* are wrong? What if I'm the poor one percent whose operation is not a complete success? By this time tomorrow I could lose my sight! Then what? Do I then go to the press, or go on television, and declare to the world that *they* don't know what they're talking about?"

He checked himself and realised that his wife was just trying to help, that she was most probably correct as usual and that he was simply being over-sensitive. Realising that he had raised his voice to his wife, an occurrence that was alien to both of them, he put his hand gently on her arm and whispered, "Sorry, Pam."

After a brief pause, he turned his gaze back to the window, sipped some tea and wondered aloud, "You know, every day of my life I've opened my eyes and focused on the day before me."

"Apart from last birthday, when the only thing that helped you focus in the morning was a strong black coffee!" she chuckled.

"Yes," he continued, seemingly unaware of her intention, but allowing a grin to acknowledge the interjection. "But what if…you know…I mean, how would someone cope if heaven forbid they were to wake up one day and see, well darkness, like our garden right now?"

They both took a moment to pause at the conjecture. What a terrible thought. How awfully sudden it would be. Noticing his wife's eyes slowly beginning to close, he broke the silence by suggesting that she go back to bed, which she dutifully did, although not without a trace of guilt as she left him alone to contemplate the silence.

By five-thirty Mr Tanner had dressed, put on a long overcoat and was now walking along Old South Head Road, facing the steep incline leading to Victoria Road. As he approached the brow of the hill he marvelled as Cooper Park came into view, with its beautiful array of trees silhouetting against a dawn that was simply breathtaking. Huffing and puffing, with his fists on his hips, he patiently waited for the sun to rise on the horizon. A crisp, winter breeze made him button his coat on this cool July morning. A line of cars was already snaking its way towards the city as workers were busily trying to miss the rush hour, and he considered himself lucky since he had booked in his annual holiday to coincide with his eye appointment.

Just as his mind began wandering back to thoughts of eye surgery, white coats and an uncertain future, he was jolted back to reality as the crown of a stunning sun could be seen appearing above reddish-purple clouds in the distance. He stood dead still as the haze of the sun shimmered and continued steadily rising above the Sydney skyline. 'What an amazing sight!' he thought. 'What absolute, sheer beauty! And it's for free; all of it, every day! How many times must I have missed this burst of glory because I was rushing to work, or finishing a spreadsheet of accounts online before my deadline?'

The sun, now too powerful to observe with the naked eye, was rising higher and higher, and Mr Tanner decided to continue his walk, with Cooper Park on his right. He stopped at an opening, where a precipitous drop was prevented by dozens of steps leading down to a large grassy area. He stared at the trees in the distance, with their perfect green curves piercing the sky. A childish thought crept into his mind, as he imagined a giant from his early fairytale books gently bending down and effortlessly uprooting one of these huge trees and munching on it like a stick of broccoli. As the giant tucked a few extra sticks into his breast pocket for later delight, he turned and walked stealthily in the direction of Sydney harbour, just missing the famous Opera House with his right heel. As he waded into the water he turned around to give Mr Tanner a farewell wave, then disappeared into the depths, never to be seen again.

Mr Tanner closed his eyes and tried to hold the image in his mind's eye, but the sound of the traffic behind him distracted his thoughts. He kept his eyes tightly shut and imagined what it must be like without sight. He could still see the sun, the trees and the skyline, but the vision lacked precision, so he opened his eyes again and this time studied the bushes in front of him. On closer inspection he saw greater detail: the luscious green of the thick leaves, the sharp points at the tips of the foliage and then, quite by chance, he caught sight of a thin, almost invisible line stretching from one point to another. He looked closely at the web spun by the black and yellow spider, which awaited its prey in the middle of the maze it had constructed. Usually the sight of this huge, eight-legged monster would have repulsed him, but today he saw it as a stroke of genius, a work of art. 'What a life!' he thought, 'to have to work so hard and wait until some poor, unfortunate mite becomes ensnared in your trap until you slowly devour it, only to start the whole process again before your next meal!'

Feeling relieved to belong to the class of homo sapiens, he hurried along to the crossroads which housed not only the complex system of traffic lights, but also the solitary man who scratched a living every day by offering to clean the windscreens of drivers who appeared reluctant to oblige. Mr Tanner watched as the familiar face of the man with the ginger beard weaved between cars, with a pleading look in his eyes, only to be met in the main by a hostile audience who either simply shook their heads, or fists, or both. As he was waiting for the lights to change, Mr Tanner began wondering how the bearded man faced each day, dealing with the thousands of negative would-be customers in his open-air office. Did the man have a home? What did he do with the money he was given by the charitable few who allowed him to wash their already clean windscreens? How must he feel each hour, as each change of the lights brought him a shower of abuse, scorn or pity? What did he do before this? Had he lost his job? Was he once a well-paid executive who one day found himself out on the streets?

As the lights changed and Mr Tanner drew closer to the windscreen cleaner, he hesitated, put his hand in his pocket and fiddled with a two-dollar coin between his thumb and index finger. 'Would this cause offence?' he wondered. Would he receive a clout from a man already frustrated with a condescending public? Mr Tanner contemplated the possibility of never seeing this man again, so, with an air of confidence, he approached him, smiled and said quite simply, "I'm sorry. You missed my car the other day. Would you accept this?"

The windscreen cleaner broke into a huge smile, laughed aloud and threw his head back, as he replied, "Good on yer, mate! You have a great day now!"

Mr Tanner wasn't exactly sure which one of them was the recipient of charity, and began feeling slightly embarrassed. Was the man laughing at him now? Would he tell all his friends about some 'pathetic guy' who thought he might be helping the world by giving a windscreen cleaner a measly two dollars? But then again, did it really matter? Mr Tanner smiled to himself, felt he had done the right thing and moved swiftly on.

By now, a few dark clouds had begun to move in from the east, and the likelihood of rain had increased. He tried walking a few steps with his eyes closed but quickly lost confidence, so sat down in a bus shelter, hands on his lap with his face to the wind. Again he closed his eyes. He could hear the sound of the city, the distant hum of an aeroplane no doubt on its way to some faraway country, and the patter of hurried footsteps on the pavement. Each of these sounds told him a story, and he tried to imagine all the lives of the people either in the air or on the ground. The more he concentrated the more he 'saw' through sound: the squeaking of a pram wheel; a rainbow lorikeet that had just taken flight from a nearby bush; an impatient driver; the click-click of a young woman in high heels (he never did understand how people could walk in such shoes!); the rustle of a bag that had just been put by his leg, and its large owner who sat next to him, and who clearly needed more room than the average person. With greater concentration he even heard his own breathing and for the first time in his life he appreciated that his breathing was always on 'automatic pilot', so to speak. 'What if', he thought, 'we somehow had to operate our breathing manually? It just happens, day and night, twenty-four seven!'

Soon he felt people standing up, probably in anticipation of an oncoming bus. Sure enough, the screeching of brakes and the hiss of automatic doors told him that he had guessed correctly, and he felt proud that he was able to manage at least for some time without the use of his sight. The sound of two pairs of feet running at great speed alerted him to some sense of urgency, and as he heard a breathless, middle-aged woman calling out, "Come on, hurry up! Be quick!" he couldn't bear the suspense and had to interrupt his game to see the scene. Alas, the doors closed, the bus sped off with a roar and the mother and son were left stranded at the bus stop. Clearly, the young boy was about to apologise, but was unable as the mother started a barrage of verbal abuse in front of Mr Tanner and those waiting for a different number. The boy looked embarrassed as the mother directed her frustration at him, using adjectives such as "stupid" and "useless," then finding it necessary to explain to everyone how he "…was always late" and how he always held her up. Her final attack announced that it was his fault that they had missed their bus.

As another bus followed just five minutes after, and as they climbed onto it with mother shaking her head and pushing her son onto the step while she searched in her purse for the correct fare, Mr Tanner considered pointing out to her that perhaps the earlier bus was not in fact their bus after all, and that this was the bus they were meant to board. If he had had the courage, he then would have asked her whether the extra five minutes was worth the public humiliation of her son. Here he was, on the brink of an operation that could change his life, and just now a young boy had been flogged in public because of a few extra minutes at a bus shelter.

Walking away from the crime scene, Mr Tanner reflected on the sounds he had heard and reasoned with himself that if, awful as it would be, his sight went, at least he still had his hearing.

He had not noticed, with all this activity, the time ticking by, and the deterioration of the weather. Looking up, he now saw darker clouds appearing like grey cotton wool, and he started making his way back home with his eyes still fixed on the sky. For a while he quickened his step. Feeling the rain on his neck he grunted "Oh no, drizzle!" but then stopped and thought how much more accurate the French rendition of 'drizzle' -'la pluie fine' -

'fine rain', depicted this short cloudburst. As he pulled his collar up he remembered an old favourite song, and found himself humming a line from it: *'I turned my collar to the cold and damp'*. He felt it a privilege to have been able to hear such wonderful music during his life and pondered on the millions of songs that had been written with a scale of only seven notes.

Just then, a horrible thought struck: 'What if I were to lose my hearing as well?' He trembled as he felt himself slipping into a downward spiral of helplessness, and he experienced a pang of guilt as he realised how often he took these senses for granted. Reaching his favourite local coffee shop, he paused, shut his eyes, pressed his thumbs against his ears and tried to imagine life without the use of both sight and sound. It was a depressing notion and it frightened him. He couldn't bear the thought of it and, try as he may, he was unable to keep up the tormenting game of 'see-nothing-hear-nothing'. He looked around and brought his hands quickly to his sides. He peered inside the coffee shop and saw people enjoying breakfast. The delicious smell of freshly-ground coffee relaxed him and he comforted himself with the thought that all was well, he could still see, hear, smell and almost taste the hot steamy coffee in the polystyrene cups.

With the 'pluie fine' now turning into heavy droplets of rain, he walked faster until he reached the corner of Victoria Road. "Another ten minutes" he said to himself. "Then I'll be home and dry and can prepare myself for the appointment." But then he stopped. Why, he wondered, did he have to run back home? He had spent the last hour or so appreciating everything around him. What was so 'gloomy' about grey clouds? Was there not a beauty in those, too? He paused, in the middle of the rain, to give himself time to remember the sunrise, the broccoli-eating giant, the spider, the bearded windscreen cleaner, the pram wheel and the coffee shop. He felt a warm tear trickle down his left cheek, and wasn't sure whether it was the wind or just his sheer joy in being alive. But it didn't matter. He *was* alive, he *did* have his sight, he *could* hear the symphony of life around him and he wanted to use every possible moment to enjoy it. He walked even faster, then broke into a jog, not because of the rain or the wind, but because he wanted to cherish every moment with his dear wife. A rush of emotion overcame him as he ran faster and faster, trying to take in everything as he dashed past houses, motor scooters, an abandoned shoe and a stray dog, each with a story of its own. He laughed as he felt the now heavy rainfall on his head, and he pulled off the thick-rimmed glasses which no longer served any purpose.

Arriving at his front door, he wiped his eyes dry, partly from the rain and partly from his tears. The front hall now had a small puddle around his feet, but instead of taking off his wet clothes and darting for the shower, he called up excitedly, "Pam! Pam! Come on, hurry up! Be quick!" and the irony of the imperative made him chuckle.

His wife came running to the top of the stairs and said in a tone of some alarm, "What's the matter? What's happened?" He looked up at her and was thankful that she had already dressed.

"Come down, I want to introduce a very important guest to you!" he said in haste. His wife quickly descended the staircase and stood in front of her husband, now dripping even more rainwater on the parquet floor. "It's a guest you've never met before, and you'll never meet again," he added enigmatically.

His wife stared at him, blinking in confusion and looked behind him to see who was there. "Who's the guest?" she asked in bewilderment seeing nobody behind him or anywhere near him.

"Today!" he said triumphantly. "Come on, put your coat on, let's go out!"

His wife, unsure of his present state of mind, spoke tenderly and pointed out, "But it's pouring."

"Yes," he acknowledged.

"But it's cold," she added.

"Yes," he simply replied.

"Listen, why don't you dry off, have a shower and I'll make you some hot tea. We've still got plenty of time before the appointment. Perhaps we'll go out tomorrow."

"What tomorrow? What if there is no tomorrow? Imagine this was our last day."

Mrs Tanner glared at him. "Whatever are you talking about?"

Mr Tanner raised an eyebrow, which meant that he was about to say something of great importance. "What time is it?" he quizzed.

"Seven thirty-eight, to be precise," she said, reading the numbers from her digital watch.

"There will never be another seven thirty-eight on this Monday morning again. Never!"

As they locked the door behind them they ran out into the street, under a large golfing umbrella, and walked to the coffee shop. His wife, starting to feel a little awkward but not wanting to upset him on this significant day, pleaded, "You know, it's still raining hard and we're getting really wet out here. Why don't we go and have some coffee? We can dry off, have a chat and plan…" She was stopped in her tracks by an event she had never experienced and, frankly, did not know how to respond to. She thought a huge truck must have turned the corner and ran over a massive puddle, for her long coat was suddenly drenched, and her shoes were now flooded with water. When she looked at her husband, however, she understood differently, for there he was, grinning from ear to ear, eyebrow raised and shrugging his shoulders.

"What, what on earth are you…?" she began, but before she could finish, he raised his leg for the second time, cocked his head then plunged his foot once again into the huge puddle, soaking both him and his wife. A little child and her mother looked on in shock. Mrs Tanner felt a mixture of powerlessness and rage, but when she looked at the little girl, wide-mouthed, then saw her husband heaving with laughter, she felt an uncontrollable desire to retaliate. Leaping suddenly into the air, she came down with a double attack, as she landed with both feet in the centre of the puddle. At that moment, an elderly lady was scurrying towards them, wondering what all the fuss was about. With no umbrella of her own, she was clutching her shopping bag, trying to dodge the human traffic and take some shelter under shop blinds whenever she could. Mr Tanner remembered the classic scene in 'Singing in the Rain' and, overacting with great chivalry, offered his umbrella to the lady, gave his best Gene Kelly smile, then tap-danced between the gutter and the pavement. By now, more onlookers were gathered, and the Tanners were holding on to each other, laughing more than they had for ages.

The operation took just an hour. Mr Tanner was now more serious as the bandages were slowly being unwrapped around his head. He heard voices speaking about mundane matters, which gave him some confidence that this was routine and that there was nothing to worry about. The blanket on the bed felt soft, like the teddy bear he used to have when he was a boy. The odour of hospital filtered through his nostrils and a sickly taste remained in his mouth as a result of the anaesthetic. He felt an anticlimax as he opened his eyes, expecting a darkened room, blinds drawn, with concerned faces looking at him through large magnifying glasses. He also anticipated a blurred view and giddiness which was bound to follow after such an operation. Instead, he opened his eyes to a bright ward, prettily decorated, with doctors and nurses moving here and there. A spray of rhododendrons had been placed in a vase next to his bed. He sat still and looked down at the cream-coloured sheet beneath his hands. He breathed a deep sigh and saw the shadow of a man in a long coat approach his bed.

"Thank you," he whispered in hushed reverence.

"You're most welcome, Mr Tanner," said the doctor who was smiling at his successful patient. Mr Tanner looked up at the doctor and quietly whispered,

"Thank you, too." The doctor looked a little confused but put it down to post-anaesthetic disorientation. After a perfunctory glance at the record sheet hanging over the foot of the bed, the doctor nodded with a smile, then walked to the next bed and engaged in conversation with a man still bandaged around the head.

Mr Tanner breathed slowly and deeply in gratitude. In the last twenty-four hours he had learnt how to look, not just see; he had experienced the wonder of listening, rather than simply hearing. He had become more aware than ever before of his surroundings, and had marvelled at the world's beauty, from the expanse of the sky to the delicate thread of a web. Soon he would leave the hospital and be reunited with his wife. But could he go back to his ordinary life, in his ordinary house, the same person he was yesterday? He pondered over these thoughts as he drifted into a light doze, unaware that his wife had entered the ward to take him home.

That night, after talking to his wife about the day's experiences, he hopped into bed and drew the blanket towards him. His wife, relieved for both of them, went to pull the light cord above their bed, when she noticed his clock.

"Darling," she said, "Look, you've left the alarm on at four o'clock!"

"I know," he grinned, and then, switching off the light himself, turned over and fell into a deep, relaxing sleep.

Sarah's Doll

Sarah loved her doll. She loved to take it out of the old, tattered box and look at her. She loved dressing her and bathing her. But most of all, she loved to cradle her in her arms, rock her gently to sleep and sing to her. When her father had brought home the box with the bright yellow ribbon and Sarah had marvelled at the contents inside, she set out straight away to give her new doll a name. She had considered 'Baby Blue Eyes', 'Victoria' and other such names as her friends had given their dolls. But, unable, or simply unwilling to do things just because others did, she settled quite quickly on 'Dolly'.

Now she sat up in bed, straightening Dolly's dress. It reminded her of the dress daddy had bought her on her birthday: blue, puff sleeves and white lace at the hem. She loved the way the dress swirled around her when she span around in a twirl, imagining she was in a ballroom dancing with a young prince. Daddy was her prince. She loved daddy and the way he made such a fuss of her. Mummy was so kind and generous, and gave her all the love and attention she could wish for; but daddy used to spoil her and, at bedtimes, when mummy would ask daddy to put her to bed, "calmly and without any fuss," he would whisk her upstairs, do a funny jig they had made up together, then read her stories until he fell asleep!

Dolly's deep blue eyes stared into Sarah's, and Sarah tried to get Dolly off to sleep by tilting her gently backwards until her little eyes closed. She giggled when Dolly's eyes flickered open again as soon as she was sitting up straight again in Sarah's arms. 'I wonder how much sleep a baby needs,' Sarah thought. She looked at her reflection in the mirror opposite and saw that her face looked puzzled. Pictures were popping up in her head but she couldn't quite put them together. In one of the pictures she saw a baby laughing as he spat out a dummy. In another a baby was sleeping to the sound of a young mother singing a lullaby. In yet another she saw a baby screaming with a bright red face. She didn't like this one bit, and so decided to put an end to the pictures and look again at peaceful Dolly with her combed hair looking so neat and tidy.

Sarah stroked Dolly's hair. It was chocolate brown. Sarah liked chocolate, even though she was often told that too much was not good for her. She stared again in the mirror and exposed her teeth. They were in good order, clean and straight, so why shouldn't she eat chocolate? Chocolate made her feel nice. Why was everyone telling her what to do? She looked down again at Dolly and played with the safety-pin that was attached to the front pocket of the dress. Then she looked at the little piece of paper that was pinned onto it. She ran her fingers slowly over the words written in black felt-tip: 'We love you'. She struggled to remember when the note was written or indeed who had written it. She gave up after a while and was just comforted by the fact that it made her feel warm and safe.

The heat of the room made her feel thirsty, and as she turned her head she noticed a small beaker of orange juice on her bedside table. She saw a beige flap-over folder on the cabinet. Someone had written her name on the folder. There were also three large letters in capitals just under her name, but from where she was sitting she couldn't make them out. Some papers were peeping out from the folder, but they were just out of reach. Something inside her made her want to read the papers but she could not get to them without letting go of Dolly, and she wasn't prepared to do that. Not just yet. She wasn't ready.

The juice was cool and soothing. She drank it so quickly that a trickle ran down her chin and onto Dolly's dress. Now the dress had an orange stain on it. Never mind, it would wash in the machine, provided the label didn't state that it had to be hand-washed. She wondered how she knew that. 'Must have read about it or someone must have told me,' she said to herself.

Suddenly she was aware that the door-knob was slowly turning and that somebody was about to come in. She quickly hid Dolly under the bedcovers. They had taken her away once before, and she wasn't about to let them do it again. She closed her eyes and pretended to be resting. She heard soft footsteps on the tiled flooring and then felt a hand rest gently on hers.

"Sarah," the voice said gently, "It's time to go." She sighed and slowly opened her eyes. She turned her head slightly to the right and saw her husband's loving, moist eyes looking directly at her. Next to him were Rachael, smiling at her mother and little Ben, who was not sure whether to laugh or cry.

"The baby's fine. He's at home. You've had a shock. It's been three weeks. Come on home now, we all need you."

A kaleidoscope of images and memories flashed before her. Now she remembered: the dark clouds; the ambulance; the fears; the tears. She looked at her family and whispered, "I'm sorry, I'm so sorry."

"It's fine, come now," her husband said reassuringly.

As she slipped on her dressing gown and slippers she glanced at the folder. She did not understand what the letters 'PND' meant; neither did she wish to know. All she knew was that she was getting better, that she had a wonderful family and that she was going home. On reaching the door she stopped, turned around and said,

"Wait." She walked to the bed and folded back the blanket to pick up Dolly. But there was nothing there; just an orange stain on the sheets and a little note which said 'We love you'.

David, the Karate Kid

The day started off as usual at Larkswood High school for boys. The same boys came late, I had to reprimand one or two teachers for hogging the photocopier and the caretaker complained about "the disgraceful state of the school dining room!" Although I wasn't the Head, or even the Deputy, my twenty years of service at the school had gained me the experience, and had won me the respect, of staff and students. Not that I was soft by any means - the pupils knew that I could have a good joke with them, especially the seniors, but at the same time, if they crossed that line, they'd be grounded. So it was, that after working my way up from ordinary class teacher, to Form Tutor, to Head of House and finally to Head of Year, I felt well and truly entrenched in the school and its systems, and I suppose I had resolved to stay there for the rest of my career, particularly since I had just reached a 'significant' birthday.

As well as knowing my subject rather well I was also told that I taught it in a lively way and that the pupils enjoyed my classes. I rarely raised my voice, but on the odd occasion when I needed to, they said that the booming sound would resonate around the whole school, and that kids in the lower years cowered in their classrooms when they heard 'The Jeff Farman Roar'!

My Year Group was great, and by and large we all got on really well. It's difficult sometimes to strike up a rapport with sixteen-year-olds, especially when you are twenty-five years older than the young lads, and yet, with a bit of camaraderie, and give and take on both sides, there was harmony between us.

All except for David. David had what the staff and kids called "an attitude." He was quite short, exceptionally stocky with an olive skin complexion and was always untidy. Most staff had given up telling him to tuck in his shirt, straighten his tie and to clean his shoes. Although he was not from a wealthy family you couldn't exactly call him poor, so when Ms West once attempted to fight his corner over a coffee in the staffroom as she protested, "Maybe David can't afford shoe polish or a new shirt!" she was met with laughter and disdain. That was her first and last attempt to stick up for him, particularly since he played up in her Geography class later that afternoon.

I must admit, David was a mystery to me. He walked in every day with a deep frown on his face, shoulders slightly bent and a look of anger that made the most seasoned of teachers shudder. He certainly was a tough nut. By the age of eleven he had already won competitions in his favourite sport, Karate, and had broken the noses of two of our seniors. By thirteen, the kids knew to leave well alone, and they would keep close to the corridor walls whenever he walked by, with his head staring at his feet and fists clenched. By fourteen he had been awarded his black belt. His anger, along with his appalling bad temper, usually got the better of him, and more often than not he would end up either in the 'time out room' (our euphemism for 'the sin bin'), in my office or visiting the Head for "a little chat." Staff had for a long time suggested the Head give him a good hiding but the political machinery had long been oiled on that issue and corporal punishment was outlawed.

I don't know what had happened on that fateful day when the staff spoke of "the straw that broke the camel's back" but he must have done something pretty awful. The whole staffroom was buzzing about "that David again!" and a small posse had formed around the smoking table, about to draft an affidavit for his public lynching. I could see that tempers were high, staff morale was low and that something had to be done to calm the waters. Although I tried to avoid becoming involved in the affair, I had a feeling that they wanted to see blood and that I was going to be elected Chief Executioner. I pretended not to hear what they were saying and buried my face into the newspaper whilst gripping my coffee tightly.

As predicted, one of the mob approached me and said with a voice not void of emotion, "Come on, Jeff, you've got to help us out here!"

"But he's not even in my Year Group" I pleaded. "Besides, it's only one period to the bell, then we'll all be off for the weekend. It'll all die down by Monday!"

"Not this time," came the reply. "He's really done it this time. Go on, sort him out good and proper. He deserves it. We've had enough! You're the only one who can get through to him."

I have to confess I was flattered. I really didn't want a showdown. I just wanted to go home and have a relaxing evening. However, not wishing to lose face with my colleagues, I put down my mug, stretched my arms, yawned nonchalantly to give the impression that this was all in a day's work, and said with an air of finality, "Right! Let's do it! Where is he?" A small cheer was heard from around the smoking table and his Form Tutor ran off to find David as I left the staffroom and began pacing the corridor like a panther ready for the kill.

A short while later, David appeared at the doorway to the corridor, accompanied by his teacher who wore a smug expression on his face which said, "Now you're for it!"

David stood stock still, his fists clenched by his side, his frown still there and with teeth bared. I nodded to the teacher and he left the scene quickly, as if in a Western shoot-out. I said nothing but simply beckoned David to come to me which, surprisingly, he did straight away. Aware of a few pupils and staff watching from the stairs, I felt the curtains opening for the matinee performance and, with one hand on my hip and the other pointing upwards I yelled "Get up those stairs!"

David showed no emotion but obediently followed orders as he slowly ascended the stone stairs to my office on the top floor. When we reached halfway I felt he should realise again who was in control, and so I followed up with a "Move it!" His pace did not quicken and I did not want to lose grip of the situation so I decided to let this pass without further comment. As we reached the top of the stairs he thrust his hands into his pockets and fixed his eyes firmly ahead of him. I realised that, big as I was, he could have floored me with one swipe. I'd seen those knobbly knuckles and knew that, in spite of his height, he was extremely strong for his age. I therefore kept a safe distance in case he lost control of himself and took a swing at me, thus landing me in hospital and him in court.

"Sit down, there!" I commanded. He walked to a table, kicked one of the legs of a chair, and then slumped into one of the black plastic chairs. This was the moment everyone had waited for - the 'Farman Level Three Blast', enough to crack the toughest of them. I stood behind him, looking at his unkempt, jet-black hair. I wasn't sure whether I should build up to a crescendo or just let him have the lot at once. I decided on the latter, and thought that the sudden release of decibels would shock him into submission. I slowly drew breath, quietly and steadily so he would not hear and be prepared for the jolt, and when I felt that my lungs were finally full of air paused just a second to release my venom onto him.

To this day I don't know why I changed tack. Just as I was about to blast him, and impress my colleagues on the stairwell, I hesitated, and then, almost unwittingly, in a very soft voice asked, "David, are you happy?" I shall never forget the scene that unfolded; neither shall I ever cease being grateful that I did what I did. David took his hands out of his pockets, cradled his head on his arms and jerked forward with his arms on the desk in front of him. I would say that he then started to cry, but he didn't. He sobbed and sobbed, like a baby, barely able to catch his breath. I stood and watched in shock. He ran his hand through his hair, then buried his head again into his arms, still weeping incessantly.

I wasn't sure what to do or what to say, but when eventually I did muster up enough courage to speak I asked, "David, what is it? What's the matter?"

Controlling himself as best as he could he then proceeded to tell me about his home: how he had to go back every night and help with his handicapped brother; how he needed to be there to look after him, wipe up the mess, feed him and to try to keep him clean; how he tried to help his mother with the housework because she had been working closely with the physiotherapist all day to try to see some improvement in his brother's condition, and how he desperately tried to stay up night after night to finish his homework, late into the early hours of the morning, in order to succeed in his exams so that he could get a good job and earn enough to look after his kid brother.

As he continued crying I just stood and trembled. I then, for the first time in my professional career, broke the golden rule. I crouched down next to this brave young teenager, put my arms around him and cried with him. When we had both reached a point where we could shed no more tears I looked at him, gripping his arm and gently said, "David, all these years, why didn't you ever say anything to us?" He looked at me without an ounce of malice and simply replied, "You never asked."

David left school at the end of that year, achieving average success in his exams. We didn't know what happened to him, where he went or what he did for a living. But he did teach us that, with all our academic degrees and professional qualifications, at the heart of teaching is the child, and that there is more to teaching than curriculum. If we want children to listen to us, and what we have to teach them, we first have to listen to them. Although I still feel ashamed of our treatment of

David, I shall always be grateful to him for teaching us that children don't care how much we know until they know how much we care.

The Bee

Once there was a bee. It was an ordinary worker bee. It buzzed merrily in the meadow and pollinated the beautiful white flowers which grew there. The bee did not know the name of the flowers, nor did it need to – it was just a bee. The flowers flourished and gave off a powerful, sweet fragrance. They were very attractive indeed.

Lucy was the farmer's daughter. Three times a week Lucy rode her bike from the farm to the meadow where she picked beautiful white flowers for her father to take to market, along with the eggs, milk and cheese he collected from the farm. Lucy loved the ride to the meadow, even when it rained, and the sight of all those pretty white flowers made her feel good.

Lucy's father had a first name, but everyone called him

'Farmer' and he didn't mind this one bit. When he went to the market very early in the morning he would sell his eggs, milk, cheese and pretty white flowers to the market people, who took their goods to the city. Reg bought the flowers from Farmer and drove his small van fifty miles to spend the whole day sitting at his flower stall outside the train station.

Alex lived with his unmarried sister, Beth, in the house they had inherited from their parents. Alex was younger than Beth, and he loved her very much indeed. He so longed for her to be married. Every Friday he would come out of the station and buy Beth flowers for the weekend. She particularly liked the white flowers he bought from Reg, the flower man at the station. Alex did not know the name of the flowers, nor did he need to – he was a regular customer and Reg always put aside a bunch for him.

Beth worked as a stockbroker in the city. She was very good at her job and enjoyed it very much. She loved her brother but spent much of her time wishing she were married and that she could start a home of her own one day. She adored the flowers Alex bought her and decided she would make him feel good by placing one delicately in her hair. She looked in the mirror and thought it rather attractive, so she left it in one day as she went to the Stock Exchange. The white flower looked very pretty and blended well with her soft, fair hair.

The Stock Exchange is a very busy hive of activity indeed. Hundreds and hundreds of people work there, rushing here, rushing there, keeping their eyes glued to screens to see the prices of the latest stocks and shares. Nobody has much time for anything else at the Stock Exchange and the workers there often do not see anything, or anyone, except for the screens. The people are very smart and wear neat suits, skirts and polished shoes. Most people do not see the clothes, though, as their eyes are often either looking down at the floor, or watching the screens on the walls. Once, though, while Martyn was trying to squint at a screen on the wall, his eye caught something pretty and white in someone's hair. He had never seen a woman wear a flower in her hair. He did not know the name of the flower – nor did he need to, for as he walked closer to the flower he could smell its sweet fragrance and his attention then turned to the warm, kind face beneath the flower. Martyn and Beth started chatting and became friends.

At their wedding, Martyn and Beth both wanted the same pretty white flowers that had first brought them together. The wedding was stunning. There was much laughter, dancing and happiness. Everybody said that they made the perfect couple and Alex was absolutely delighted for his sister. Very shortly after, Martyn became very successful at the Stock Exchange and so he and Beth were very wealthy in a very short time. Beth let Alex keep the house they had inherited from their parents and so everybody was very happy.

When Beth had her first baby they were so excited, and all of their relatives and friends were excited for them. When Beth came out of the hospital she and Martyn invited everybody to a party to celebrate the birth of their baby. They decorated the house with balloons, coloured napkins and lace tablecloths. Everyone was there, and they all noticed the pretty white flowers that were placed on all of the tables. People commented on the flowers, but few knew what they were called – they did not need to, because so much else was going on around them. However, Beth's brother, Alex, stood by himself in a corner and looked at all the people, so happy because of the celebration to which they had been invited. Even some of the guests were now wearing the pretty white flowers – in the lapels of their suit jackets or in their hair, just like Beth.

A few minutes before Martyn made his speech, Alex walked up to him and Beth and mentioned how strange it was that something as simple as a pretty white flower could have brought about such happiness. The three of them stared at each other for a moment. By the time Martyn finished his speech, everyone was grateful for the meeting he and Beth had had at the Stock Exchange; they were grateful to Beth for wearing the flower in her hair, which first attracted Martyn; to Alex for buying the flowers; to Reg for sitting outside the station at his flower stall; to Farmer for bringing the flowers to the market, and even to Lucy for picking the flowers……..but nobody thought of the bee.

The Elevator

Don Randall had just left his favourite shop and was now running to catch the bus which would take him to his apartment on 42nd Avenue. His luck was in, or the New York bus driver was just feeling unusually kind that day. His latest purchase came with a receipt, and he put both in his jacket pocket, along with his wallet, keys and a selection of knick-knacks he had not bothered to deal with over the week.

A single man in his thirties, Don worked mostly nights, so he made use of the daytime to catch up on shopping, going to the bank, visiting museums or just sitting in the park and relaxing. He was a tall man with neat, black hair and a well-trimmed moustache. Although not a great lover of fashion he did like to look smart, and that sometimes meant buying a suit that would fit in with the style of the time.

When he left the bus, which fortunately for him stopped right outside his apartment, he walked in to the building, just in time to see the elevator doors closing. "Hold 'em!" he called out, and one of the two occupants must have felt sorry for him, as just before the doors met one another, they re-opened, allowing him to join the young woman and man inside.

"Thanks," he puffed, and was acknowledged by a nod from the woman. He pressed the button for the twelfth floor, then let out a "Phew!" to indicate that he was grateful for her benevolence. The elevator climbed slowly, floor by floor, and he began to think of how he was going to set about tidying up his apartment. 'OK, should I start with the bedroom or the kitchen?' he mused, but his thoughts were rudely interrupted when the elevator came to a sudden halt between the fourth and fifth floors.

"Heck, not again!" he exclaimed with an air of frustration. "Second time this week!"

He could see that the woman was looking a little nervous, so he let out a little laugh to try to break the ice. The other man in the elevator was also looking quite on edge, with his hands in his pockets and his head facing the floor, and so Don turned to him and said, "Hey, buddy, don't worry. We'll just alert the emergency services and they'll have us out in twenty minutes or so."

As he went to press the emergency button, the man snapped, "Don't touch that!"

"What are you talking about?" asked Don.

"Never mind," the man curtly answered. "I'll make my own way out of here!"

With that, the man looked up at the ceiling and tried to reach a panel that led to the lift shaft.

Don and the woman looked on incredulously as the man became quite agitated trying to unscrew the panel with his fingers. The screws were obviously only thumb-tight as they appeared to be turning quite easily.

"You really don't have to do that, and besides you'll probably get hurt," Don continued.

"Shut up!" the man hissed. "If you don't, you're the one likely to get hurt!"

The woman started crying and Don, lifting himself to his full height, and with a deep frown, said, "Hey, that's enough! I'm calling the services whether you like it or not!" and with that, he stretched out his arm to press the button.

Before he could, he felt a heavy blow come down on his wrist, and he let out a cry of pain. He span around to see the woman with her eyes closed and hands over her ears, and the man holding a small gun in his right hand. The man was sweating and his hand was shaking slightly. His breathing quickened and his teeth were clenched.

"You asked for it, pal," he barked, and he pointed the gun directly at Don. The woman momentarily opened her eyes and was about to scream, when the man stifled her by standing behind her and covered her mouth with his hand.

"Hey, what are you...?" began Don, but the man put the gun to the woman's head and shouted, "Shut up I said! I don't want no emergency services here, swarming with cops. You're in my way, now you're both gonna get it! See this attachment? It's a silencer. Nobody will hear the shots. I'll get through the lift shaft and nobody will be the wiser!"

The man seemed to enjoy the power he held at that moment, so, relishing the position he held, he pointed the gun towards the lift buttons and pulled the trigger twice. He was right - the silencer only let out two dull thuds. The elevator circuit board sparked and there was a hole where the emergency button had been. Now no-one would know that they were in an elevator with a gun-wielding maniac.

"There," he mumbled, "that should keep them away for a while. Now, for you two. I bet you wish you never came in here today!" he laughed as only a madman would. Suddenly, Don had an idea.

"Are you a gambling man, then?" he asked, trying to make his voice sound as calm as he possibly could.

"What?" the man asked.

"Well," Don continued, grateful for a delay in the execution. "You say you bet we never came in. I bet that you're willing to gamble with our lives."

"What's your game?" the man asked, impatient but curious to know what was at stake.

"Look," said Don. "You're going to get out of here free either way, but the variable is whether we get out dead or alive. Ever played Russian roulette?"

The woman, who by now had been released of the gunman's grip, was not sure whether to curse the man or Don. Her mouth gaped open and her eyes stared widely at both of them. She moved her lips as if to speak, but nothing came from them.

Don capitalised on the moment's silence and carried on with an air of apparent confidence, "Look, I like to live on the edge and I thrill to a bit of danger. Last year I did my first sky dive and…"

"Get on with it before I really lose my temper!" the gunman interjected with clear annoyance.

"Okay, okay, I'm getting there. Look, don't just kill us. At least give us a fighting chance. Why don't we flip for it, like in a game of Russian roulette? You win, you shoot. We win, you escape through the lift shaft and we escape at least with our lives when the services eventually come and get us out of this place. Let's just flip for it!"

"Are you crazy?" The woman had finally found her

voice. "I'm not your toy to play with! This guy's serious and I'm not ready to die over a flipped coin!"

Although clearly agitated, the woman was surprisingly articulate. There was another silence as the man looked at the two of them and rubbed his chin. After a moment's thought he said, "Okay, why not?"

"No!" the woman shouted, but Don was now the one to quieten her. "Look, lady, we haven't got a choice. His way we both die. Our way we have a fifty-fifty chance."

At that point the woman broke down in tears, turned her back to the men and buried her face in her hands against the wall of the elevator.

"What's it to be?" Don asked calmly, "heads or tails?"

"Flip the coin!" the man ordered. Don fumbled in his pocket and brought out a shiny coin. The woman turned around and stared at his hand and the coin that would decide their fate. Don quickly placed the coin on his index finger and, with his thumb, flicked the coin into the air.

"Heads!" the man said sharply.

As the coin made its return journey to Don's palm the woman gasped and clutched her chest. Don went to catch the coin but it slipped through his fingers and landed on the floor.

"Sorry," he said, "I guess I'm nervous. Let me try again."

He took the coin for the second time, closed his eyes and drew a deep breath, after which he flipped it into the small confines of the elevator.

'Tails!" the gunman shouted, and this time the coin landed firmly in Don's left palm, whereupon he slapped the coin on the top of his right hand. His fingers gripped his right hand tightly and perspiration could be seen on his temples.

"No! No! Don't do it!" the woman begged, crying again, pleading to any sense of decency the gunman might have possessed.

"Take your hand off!" the gunman commanded.

"Look," Don said softly. "Maybe we should all just calm down. She's right, life can't be gambled away by the flip of a coin."

"Too late, buddy," the gunman grinned. "This is your bet, remember?"

At that point, Don's eyes welled up with tears, too, and he gave the gunman one last imploring line. "Please," he said, "just let us go, we haven't done anything to you."

"Show me the coin now or I'll finish this off, win or lose!"

Don looked at the woman with sorrowful eyes, let out a heavy sigh, then slowly lifted his left hand to reveal the coin underneath.

"You got lucky this time," the gunman sneered as he saw the shiny coin. With that, he stood on tiptoe, removed the panel, hoisted himself through the hole in the ceiling and started making his way up the lift shaft.

When the ambulance arrived to take Don and the woman to the hospital for shock, they passed a squad of police cars that had lined the street. Don caught a glimpse of the gunman in the back of one, handcuffed and glaring out of the window. He resisted the temptation to grin at him and wave and instead turned his attention to the woman sitting next to him who was still shaking from the ordeal.

"I thought they were going to put the security cameras in the elevator *next* month," he said, attempting to coax her into speaking. "Makes a change for them to be ahead of schedule!" he laughed. He bent his head, looked at the woman and asked, "You okay?"

"Just," she replied. "But I've got to say that my heart nearly stopped when you made that bet. Whatever made you think of doing that?" she wondered aloud, almost to herself.

Don thrust his hand into his pocket and brought out the coin. He held the coin in the flat of his hand. She saw the 'heads' side which had saved their lives, then she let out a gasp as Don turned the coin to reveal 'heads' on the other side, too. When Don showed her his 'Magic Circle' membership card and the crumpled receipt for the new coin from 'The Magician's Haven', she laughed, and then cried, through sheer relief.

The Fiddler

Leicester Square, Saturday night, outside the Odeon cinema. I'll never forget it. It really was the place to be. Tourists from all over the world who had come to see London, with its bright lights, theatres and lively restaurants, would make sure they'd book in a film at the Odeon Leicester Square. The largest cinema in Europe, its impressive black granite façade and blue neon lights dominated the Square. After a mesmerising view of the famous 'Drink Coca Cola' sign in Piccadilly Circus, they'd all come to the Square and patiently queue up outside before the doors opened for the latest feature film.

Not that I went myself. I couldn't. I spent every Saturday night working just a few yards away at the restaurant. 'Alpino's' it was called. Best Italian restaurant in town. Good food, great atmosphere and a licensed bar.

That's where I came in – a lot of the film-goers would queue to get in there after the film, and as it was so popular they felt that a bouncer on the door would steer likely bar brawlers away and attract a more conservative clientele.

So there I'd be, standing outside all on me lonesome in all weathers, with my black suit, white shirt and black tie. I looked quite good if I say so myself, with 'the Brylcreem bounce' in my hair smartly combed back and my two large gold rings on each index finger, just to remind those stupid enough to try it on that the jewellery wasn't there for show, if you know what I mean!

Now don't get me wrong. I'm not the rough type, not really. I just happen to have been born at ten pounds three and haven't stopped growing! School was fun as I could get on with my work without ever being bothered by the class bullies. I don't think I ever abused my size, or boxing training, but it stood me in good stead, especially on those exciting nights in London.

Anyway, you might think I got bored standing outside Alpino's all night. But you're wrong. You see, more than the flash Porsches and silver-painted Rolls Royces that drew up outside the cinema, I was fascinated by this poor bloke who always scraped a living by playing his violin just at the front of the queue at the Odeon. Although he was smartly dressed in his suit, tie and Trilby hat, you could see the pain in his eyes, and the embarrassment he probably felt as he wheeled himself up to the forecourt, put his violin case on the ground and started playing with such feeling. He would stay there a good hour while people were waiting for the doors to open.

He was a real gentleman, always bowing his head slightly and smiling at the street audience who would generously give him their change. Occasionally a coin would land on the patchwork blanket lying across his knees. More often than not, an adult would walk forward out of respect and place, not throw, a note into his violin case. I often wondered how much was in the case at the end of the evening. It didn't matter, though; money couldn't buy the use of this unfortunate man's legs. How did he manage to put on a brave face every week, with everyone looking at him and feeling so sorry for him?

How humiliating it must be to have to wheel yourself in front of a strange crowd and play for them, hoping they'll appreciate your music and pop something into your violin case. I was so pleased when 'Fiddler on the Roof' came out and he happily played well-known tunes from it - 'Tradition' would always attract a large crowd and receive great applause. He must have made a packet that season!

How empty, though, he must have felt, when they all disappeared into the cinema and he was left on his own, often in the cold, to pack away his instrument and wheel himself back around the corner into the darkness of night, no doubt to go back to his cold and wretched flat. I did feel for him, as no doubt others did. We sort of wanted to take him under our wing and protect him. He became a bit of a celebrity, and people who came back to see a different film enjoyed being recognised by him as he'd quip: "Didn't I see you at 'The Sound of Music'? or 'Audrey Hepburn has nothing on you, Madam!" Flattered by the familiarity, this usually drew more crowds, and more money!

So it was with a really heavy heart, one winter's night, when I saw him playing extra hard, to earn just that extra bit more and, to our dismay, the snow started falling only twenty minutes after he had begun. The concierge at the cinema realised that if the audience had to wait any longer they'd move on. He therefore decided to open the doors early and, with a "Sorry mate!" to our pitiful friend, allowed everyone in early, leaving the man in his wheelchair staring into the night, alone. He sighed, packed up his violin which he placed gently on his knees, then began wheeling himself around the corner. I desperately wanted to tell him how sorry I felt, and that he shouldn't worry because the weather was bound to be better next week, so, looking around to make sure all was quiet at Alpino's, I quickly walked after him. As I turned the corner and stared into the street dimly lit by a solitary lamp, I saw my weekly friend stop his wheelchair. He paused, no doubt to light up a cigarette. But, quick as a flash, he stood up, folded up the chair, walked to the back of the silver Rolls Royce, put chair and violin in the boot, then drove off into the night down the one-way street.

"Well, what do you know!" I chuckled to myself. "A fiddler on the fiddle!"

Route 49

"Morning, driver!"

"Morning, Russ," Frank answered, as he closed the hydraulic bus doors and pulled away from the kerb. The sun shone brightly on a beautiful September morning, and Frank was smiling, as usual, to his passengers as they boarded his bus which served the suburban Surrey green belt.

"Beautiful day today!" Russ said, leaving the correct change on the little counter next to the driver.

"Every day's a beautiful day!" Frank replied, and he watched Russ turn and laugh as he went to his seat. Russ wasn't laughing at Frank. Rather, he was chuckling because he knew that was what his friendly driver would say, and he wondered how he always managed to keep such a positive attitude when driving a bus seemed so dull and mundane.

But that was Frank Contadino. Born of Italian parents, he worked his way through school in London's East End amid xenophobic animosity, which was rife in his area, and managed somehow to emerge from it relatively unscathed. This was partly due to his parents' resolve to teach him to stand up for himself, and partly due to his thoroughly positive outlook on life, and to accept graciously whatever cards life dealt him. Where he had been willing to anglicise his forename, he steadfastly retained his surname, being quite proud of the simple farm life once led by his grandfather in Italy – hence the 'Contadino'. When he left school he had worked in various establishments, including a fast food restaurant, a video hire store and a shoe shop. He had excelled in each position, not so much because of his flair for salesmanship but more as a result of his charming, polite manner, his honesty and integrity and his ability to bring a smile to people's faces.

Now, at thirty-five, he had been driving the same bus, along the same route, for nearly four years. His line manager at the local depot had intended giving him a change, but so many passengers had commented on how pleasant their journey was, having him at the wheel, that it was put to Frank that he should continue driving bus 49 until he himself wanted to change. When approached, Frank was not bothered at all about the possibility of stagnation and boredom. In fact he rather liked building up a rapport with his regular passengers. So there he was, running the same route six days a week, with a punctuality that was envied amongst his peers.

Russ was a very successful businessman, who caught the train to his London office every morning. His mornings started with a high-powered Executive meeting in the Board Room. Russ was a stickler for timing, and anyone who arrived late for the 'Morning Exec Meet' knew that his or her position on the Executive was in jeopardy. Russ had a choice between route 47 and route 49. In fact, route 47 was slightly shorter, and would therefore get him to the station ten minutes earlier, enabling him to catch his morning coffee well in time before the departure of his train. However, having tried both routes, Russ always preferred route 49, because it was guaranteed to be on time, unlike its counterpart, and also because, "that nice driver" just gave him a 'feel good' feeling before the onslaught of the Board Room.

When Frank pulled up at the next stop he looked into his mirror at the passengers sitting patiently and called out, "Just a minute!" He called it his "driver's exercise for the day," in order to make Mrs Wheeler feel more comfortable.

Mrs Wheeler, a kind octogenarian, was finding it "…a bit difficult on the old pins" over the last few years, but she nonetheless rose early each morning to go to the local community hall to help "…those poor old people less fortunate than me." "Poor" they might have been, but many of them were Mrs Wheeler's juniors by some fifteen years. This of course never entered her head, and she walked in every day with a smile on her face "…to brighten up the place for the poor old dears."

Frank took Mrs Wheeler's shopping bag – she used to stop off to pick up a few groceries after the morning session at the hall – and let her lean on his arm as she mounted the step at the front of the bus.

"Thank you, dear," she said, as she tried to reach in her pocket for her bus pass.

"Don't worry Mrs Wheeler," Frank said, "I know you've got it."

She nodded in appreciation, then sat in the nearest available seat, while Frank scowled at the schoolboy for not getting up first, thus saving her a walk of four rows. Jumping back into his own seat, Frank called out "OK everyone, we're off!" then continued by swinging the bus around a tight hairpin bend, and up a steep hill that brought them to the scenic view at the Hog's Back, which overlooked the city, with the cathedral in the background.

Frank saw the sea of school uniforms draw closer as he slowed down. He classified the children into four categories: those who flashed their pass at him and said nothing; those who acknowledged him with at least a nod, or by raising their eyebrows; the ones who said "Hi, driver!" and his favourites, usually the younger ones, who had not yet picked up the bad habits of their elders, and said "Good morning, sir!" To some of them he was more than just the driver, he was their sounding board, even their confidant.

"You get that project finished, Jenny?" he asked one of the junior pupils who had been worried during the week.

"Not yet!" she replied with a degree of embarrassment, "But I'll be there in a couple of days...I hope!" then moved down into the bus. For some children this would have seemed an intrusion, but Jenny found it quite flattering, and even comforting, that the bus driver took an interest in her school work. She even sometimes felt more eager to please him than her own teacher at school. She knew, too, that Frank would be asking her the same question at the end of the week, so she decided to finish the project as a priority.

As Frank opened the doors for the last time that day and bid farewell to the passengers, he drove into the depot, deposited his bus keys in the drivers' box, signed out and walked home. With his key in the door, he checked himself in the reflection of the window, ensuring his tie was still straight, his crisp, clean shirt was not ruffled and that his hair was tidy. Father of two, he always wanted his wife and children to see him fresh and smart, even at the end of a long day's driving.

When the children had gone to bed, and he and his wife had washed the dishes, they sat in armchairs facing each other, drinking tea sweetened with honey.

"What is it, Frank?" his wife asked, noticing that he was deep in thought about something.

"You know, Jeanie, I wonder if you want more from me."

"What?" she asked, wondering what might have upset him that day.

"I mean, maybe I could do more, be more. We're always telling the kids to work hard so they can make something of themselves one day, and here I am, just a bus driver!"

Jean laughed, relieved that it was nothing more serious.

"No, really," he continued. "You know, I pick these people up every day. I talk to them, I even know some of their names. But to them, I'm just a bus driver. Most of them don't even acknowledge me! Some call me 'driver', or 'dear' or even 'sir', but I've got a name too! I'm Frank, Frank Contadino!"

Jean looked at him and just smiled. He would often come home and talk to her about some of the chats he had had with passengers, and she had come to know of them through his stories.

"How's that girl's project coming on?" she enquired.

"Eh? Oh Jenny, yes it's coming along," he replied, wondering whether she'd picked up the concern he had just raised.

"And that Russ man, is he still telling you how much money he's been making?"

"Not recently. He's always in such a hurry to get to that early morning meeting he holds. Mrs Wheeler's doing a bit better, though. She looked a bit more sprightly today." He stopped and looked at his wife, who was still grinning at him.

"Jeanie?" he asked, expecting her to answer his yet unformed question.

"Frank, listen," she began. "Don't you understand? You bring something new, every day, to so many people's lives.

It's not what you do that counts, it's who you are and how you do what you do. Don't you see? Mr 'Russ-money-bags' depends on you to get him to those meetings. You are partly responsible for his success. The lovely old dear does so many acts of kindness every week, but she can do that because you get her to where she needs to be. Without you on route 49 she might have to get a cab, and who knows, maybe then she wouldn't do what she does!"

Frank stared into his hot tea, took a sip, then looked at Jean to continue.

"And the school kids who turn to you and confide in you, and the people you take to work, shopping, to do sport, to meet their friends, and so on. Frank, you are not just a driver, you are *their* driver; you are 'The Driver' and nobody can do it just like you! You have your own special talents, your manner, your personality, and you touch more people's lives than you realise, just by being you. So it doesn't matter if you're a bus driver, a doctor, a banker, a secretary, a salesman or anything else – you count, and you make others feel that they, too, are counted."

"I knew I did the right thing when I married you!" he quipped.

The next morning, as the rain hammered down onto the streets of Surrey, he opened the doors to Russ, who shook his umbrella and turned down the collar of his raincoat. Frank looked at him.

"Morning, Russ. Beautiful day today!"

Russ looked through the large windscreen, the wipers frantically moving from side to side. He turned his gaze from the black, threatening clouds, put the correct change as usual onto the little counter, and then replied, "Every day's a beautiful day!"

They gave each other a friendly glance and, before moving down the bus to his seat, Russ added, "By the way, I've been meaning to ask you, what is your name?"

Frank pushed the button to close the doors, checked his mirror, indicated, then, just before pulling out, smiled at Russ and said, "Driver, just call me The Driver!"

The Grudge

"... and thou shalt not bear a grudge..."
Leviticus 19:18

Davey's eyes sparkled as they gazed into his grandmother's fireplace. Watching the glowing dance was quite hypnotic, with the yellow flames licking the logs and the crick-crack sound of dry wood being consumed by the merciless rage of the fire. He tried to follow the wisp of smoke which raced up the chimney but, crouching on his knees and craning his neck to look up he withdrew as the heat of the fire warned him that moving any closer might result in a roasting.

Sitting back on the rug in front of the hearth, Davey began rubbing a large bruise he had acquired that afternoon in the village green, when Selwyn Higgins had not only kicked him, hard, and in front of the other children, but also called him names, making those around him laugh, thus creating both physical and mental bruising. Davey smarted from the pain of the bruise on his leg, but he felt that the pain of the verbal beating would last longer.

His thoughts were interrupted by his grandmother, whom he called 'Gran', as she walked into the small front room with a large cup of hot milk and her famous home-made chocolate cake. She gently placed the tray on the little stool next to the fire, then slowly lowered herself into the rocking chair. She draped a little tartan rug on her knees and sighed.

"Now, Davey," she began. "What have you been up to, then?"

"It's that Selwyn Higgins again, Gran!" he replied, grateful for the opportunity to unwrap his hurt feelings. "He thinks he's so clever and always shows off in front of the other children, especially the girls. But you wait – you just wait until I'm a bit bigger…" He stared back into the fire and paused while he gathered his thoughts. "I'm going to plan something that will really fix him once and for all! I'll show him all right, just you see. He'll be sorry for this."

"Davey," Gran said gently, "are you going to write about it in your diary?"

Davey had been given a notebook by his father, who suggested he write down events and feelings while he was young so that one day he could reflect on them and appreciate how far he'd come. With his name written on it, and the word 'Secret' scrawled in large, black capital letters, there was no doubt that the diary was out of bounds to anyone but its owner. That notwithstanding, Davey always made sure he hid the diary in a safe place for fear that someone would find it and expose it in public. At present the diary was safely tucked in his cloth bag, which he always brought with him when visiting Gran in Pickering, a small village in the north of England.

He loved visiting Gran, not simply because she made him his favourite food, but in particular because he would ride up front with his father and mother. He would watch with care as his father harnessed the horses. Then his father would lift him high into the air and place him in the middle of the bench while his parents would sit either side of him. The journey took a good hour, and whenever Mr and Mrs Wilkes went to visit Gran, Mr Wilkes' mother, they always took butter biscuits for Davey to eat on the way. This was one of the weeks when Davey's parents allowed him to stay overnight with Gran. It was New Year's Eve, 1899, and Davey said that he preferred to be at Gran's that night, rather than be in the company of all the "…older folk, with nothing much to do." Davey was a handsome child for his eight years, and although he had already attracted the attention of some of the younger girls in the village where he lived, he was still more comfortable with Gran in her little cottage in Pickering.

Davey turned his attention to Gran. "I think," he said, "that I shall write down everything I'm going to do to Selwyn Higgins, then record how upset *he* is when it's done!"

"Now, Davey," Gran parried, "holding a grudge is not the way to live a life. You can stand up to him if you wish; you can shout back at him and call him names; you can even give him a punch on the nose if you feel like it….if you can reach!" She allowed a little chuckle to pass her lips and watched his reaction. Thankfully he smiled too. "But you must never, ever, hold a grudge, Davey, for a grudge leads only to misery."

"What do you mean, Gran?" Davey asked with his head in an inquisitive tilt.

She hesitated before responding. Born in 1840 she had had her share of misery over the years and, on this evening at the turn of the century, had little desire in burdening her grandson with the past. However, Davey, with his curly brown hair and beautiful large brown eyes, had a knack of leading her into submission and she always felt that much closer to him when she did, at last, give in. But should she give way tonight? Would the thoughts that had haunted her all these years plague him in the same way? And yet he was, after all, already working in the local stables and she convinced herself that he would have heard accounts just as terrifying from the locals.

"Gran?" he persisted. "Come on, Gran, please tell me. There's nobody here but us and I can curl up in your bed after, just like I used to when I was a littl'un! Was it that big argument no one wants to talk about between Grandad and Uncle Albert?"

She always said it was useless to try to keep it from Davey. "Young'uns know everything nowadays!" she would often repeat to Davey's parents. The night air blew through the cracks in the wooden front door, and Davey tipped another log onto the fire. Feeling that he might lose the special moment, he encouraged her by cupping the hot milk in his hands, bringing his knees to his chin so he looked good and ready for her to begin, then, with pleading eyes and a quick wink, whispered, "Go on, Gran, go on… tell me everything. I've got to know some time."

She agreed with his sentiments, bit her lip, looked towards the fire as if for inspiration, and began…

"Davey, I'm going to tell you what happened, but only to prove to you that holding a grudge can lead to, well, just about the most awful…"

"Yes, Gran, go on, please…" he interrupted.

She drew the tartan cloth closer to her chest, looked at him directly and started her story.

"I married Grandad in 1858, when I was just eighteen. Ah, Vernon Wilkes, was a fine figure of a man. All the girls in the village were terribly jealous of me, you know. He was tall and handsome and had a fiery temper which he'd unleash on anyone he felt might be giving me the eye, if you know what I mean."

Davey nodded enthusiastically. "Go on, Gran."

"Well," she continued. A couple of years after we got married I had your father. Let me see now…" She looked to the ceiling and closed her eyes. "Mmm, 1860, yes, that was the year. We had terrible snow that year and I nearly lost him as Dr. Bailey couldn't come out until late that night.

"Anyway, you've heard me talk about my dear brother, Uncle Albert. Oh, he was so good to me, even though he had such a terrible life himself, coping with his fits. He spent half his time in bed recovering from them. They were awful: he'd just lie there, as cold as the grave, without moving a muscle. Once he lay there with one eye open, and I had nightmares for ages. It could take a few hours for him to come around, and the doctor said we'd have to be careful to check him and hear his heart beat otherwise we might even think him dead! I loved him just about more than any other person in the whole world. I literally doted on him. Well, he and Grandad once had a most awful row."

"What was it about?" asked Davey, eager to hear every detail.

"You know, Davey, I'm not even sure to this day. Probably something to do with money. What I do know is that they had such a blazing row about it that they ended up screaming at each other one Sunday afternoon, just after we'd all come back from church! There I was in my Sunday best, just four years after I was married, and my husband and brother were standing just over there..." - she pointed at the pantry cupboard with wide eyes as if it were happening again right in front of her - "yelling like there was no tomorrow. Suddenly, Grandad took hold of Uncle Albert by his jacket and pulled him into the street. Everyone came out to see the two of them having a vicious fight in the village square. I cried when I saw Grandad lying by the milestone, you know the one just outside the cottage pointing to Manchester. But I also felt so bad for my brother, Uncle Albert, who was holding his chest and bleeding from his head. When Grandad stood up he shouted after Uncle Albert."

"What did he say?"

"'You'll pay for this, Albert Forrester, you see if you don't! I'll see you rot in hell if it's the last thing I do!'" she said, her voice shaking as she spoke. "Well, they never spoke to each other again and Grandad forbade me from even mentioning his name. I was awful upset, Davey, because he was my only brother, and he meant so much to me."

Again she paused and allowed the memories of the past to wash over her, so she could relate them without being a part of them. She swallowed, held back a tear, then continued. "It was 1862, I'll never forget it. Just two years after your father was born. Albert had been sending me secret letters, you know, giving them to my friend who worked at the local farm so she could slip them to me when I went to buy my milk. It was in one of those letters that he told me he was getting weaker and weaker and that the fits were getting more frequent."

She looked at Davey to add some information, but stopped to see if he was following. "You alright, Davey?" she asked, hoping he was getting tired or confused, or just plain scared.

"Oh yes, Gran, I'm fine. Do go on!"

She looked at the ceiling momentarily before continuing.

"Well, it was late one night soon after I received his last letter. Grandad was sleeping deeply and I just couldn't help myself; I sneaked out of the cottage with a thick shawl over my head and ran all the way across Wakeman's Field…"

"You ran all alone, at night, over Wakeman's?" Davey asked incredulously.

"Yes, Davey," she replied. "I was holding that very lantern over there and just prayed the light wouldn't go out. Just before I got to Uncle Albert's I saw his best friend sitting on the wall. He seemed to be crying. I shook him and asked him whatever was wrong, but when he looked up and saw me, he just cried more.

"I feared the worst and ran into Uncle Albert's cottage to find the doctor walking down the stairs. He took one look at me, shook his head and just said, "I'm so sorry, Agnes, he's had it this time."

"I don't remember running up the stairs, but the next thing I saw was him lying in bed, as still as still can be, quite lifeless. I felt his hand and it was like cold, damp wood from the forest. I screamed and screamed, then my knees gave way as I collapsed by his side, still holding his hand. The funeral took place the next morning. It was a cold, winter's day and I asked Grandad if I could go. After all, it was my brother, despite their argument. Grandad grumbled out a "Yes, if you have to," and I ran to the cemetery on the Whitby Road, just a mile from here. You know it don't you, Davey. You pass it on the way to my cottage."

Davey nodded, now transfixed by the unfolding tale.

"It was a sombre affair, with about twenty of us standing around the grave. Everybody thought the world of Albert, except Grandad of course, and we stayed right until the bell was attached."

"Bell? What bell?"

"Oh, you must have seen them, Davey. Quite a few coffins have them nowadays. They're called 'safety coffins'. The undertaker makes a little hole in the coffin and ties a string around the finger of the deceased." (She always thought 'dead' was too final and preferred the euphemism, especially when speaking to Davey). "The string passes through the hole and is threaded through a stick on top of the grave. They then attach a little bell, quite like a dinner bell used to summon maids. The bell is the last thing they put on before the funeral ceremony ends. In the past, especially with the cholera epidemic, they found that certain people had been buried alive, unintentionally, and when they woke up and discovered they were under the earth, they would pull the string which would make the bell ring. The night watchman on duty would hear the bell, come running and dig up the coffin in minutes."

Davey's face was slightly contorted. "Poor Gran, having to bury your own dead brother!"

Gran glared at Davey and said almost without moving her lips, "But that's just it, Davey," she muttered, "he wasn't! He was alive!"

At this point, Davey physically shuddered, hid his face behind his cloth bag and waited for the conclusion to this grisly tale. Suddenly, a thought ran through his logical mind. He peered over the bag and asked, "But Gran, how did they know he was alive?"

Gran's lips started to quiver and he could see a tear slowly descending her cheek. "Oh Davey, don't make me go on, child. I shouldn't have said this much already."

"No, Gran, you must, you *must*! I want to know everything once and for all."

"Davey, you must never let your parents know that I told you. Promise?"

"I promise," Davey replied, crossing his fingers behind his back.

"Oh dear, child, this is the worst bit. You see, shortly after the burial, I returned to the cottage to cook something for Grandpa, but he wasn't there. I only found out where he was when…" she hesitated.

"Yes, go on, go on!" Davey urged.

"Davey, you're not going to like this at all, but it's time you knew. Grandpa did a most terrible thing, and when he was caught, he confessed the whole story to the police. He told them how he'd followed us up to the cemetery, then waited for us to leave so he could visit the grave. Not to pay his respects, Davey, but, as he said it, "To make sure he was really and truly good and dead!" When he arrived at the grave, he stood there for a few moments and apparently he muttered some curses to my poor brother lying there stone cold beneath him. But then," she began, gripping one of the arms on the rocking chair, "a most awful thing happened, Davey. You see, Grandpa said that as he was standing at the graveside he saw the string pull the little bell! It tinkled away for a good few seconds and Grandpa realised that Uncle Albert must have woken up from his fit after all!"

She looked again at Davey who was wide-eyed and open-mouthed but this time did not wait for any interruption.

"Grandpa said that he was still filled with so much rage that, instead of alerting the watchman, he, he…" She was now choking back the tears, almost bearing the responsibility herself. "He cut the bell loose with his pocket knife, the string fell on the cold earth and Uncle Albert…" She did not need to finish. The rest of the story was clear.

Davey heaved a sigh, partly with relief that the story had ended and partly satisfied that the truth was finally out. He stared again into the flickering fire, which was beginning to die down. He noticed Gran had lifted herself out of the chair and had gone to the kitchen. He realised now why his parents had never mentioned Grandpa and the heinous crime he had committed. His mind was racing and more questions arose.

When Gran returned with a fresh cup of hot milk and another piece of cake, he nodded, took them and rested the plate on his crossed legs. He sipped some of the hot milk and tasted the delicious honey she had put in it. Then, placing his milk on the rug, asked, "But Gran, how did they find out? I mean, did Grandpa give himself up?"

"No, Davey. Early that evening the night watchman came to do his rounds and discovered the cut string and missing bell. He immediately alerted the police, who went straight to 'The Wild Boar' tavern in the village. They said it only took minutes to find the missing bell in Grandpa's jacket pocket, and that was that."

"How did they know it was the same bell?" he asked, using the logic of a veteran detective.

"Oh, that was easy. First of all, they only used little bells like that on safety coffins. But the undertaker had also scratched 'A.W.', Uncle Albert's initials on the inside of the bell."

"What happened to Grandpa?"

Again she sighed, shaking her head. In the stillness that followed they heard the celebrations beginning outside in the village. It was a macabre moment, to hear music and singing just outside a cottage where they were discussing the most gruesome details of a story that had taken place so long ago. They looked at each other again and she stared at the floor.

"Oh, Davey, it was such a long time ago. I was only young and just couldn't bear to see it all. They hanged murderers on the scaffold just outside 'The Wild Boar' and I knew immediately that this would be Grandpa's fate. I remember screaming again that day when sentence was pronounced. Some people are twisted, Davey, and they like to "go and see a good hanging!" I'd only ever seen one and it was sickening."

Davey was not sure how far to push his inquisitive mind, and so gingerly broached his next question with some trepidation. "Gran," he said quietly, "who does it? I mean, where do they find the hangman from?"

"Davey!" she exclaimed in disbelief. Then she calmed herself and realised he was just a young lad with what in fact was quite a logical question. Someone had to be the one to pull the rope for the trapdoor.

"Davey," she repeated, "that is something nobody knows. There were a few hundred people in the village, and although Grandpa may not have been the most popular of men, I cannot think for the life of me of anybody who would want to do that, even if they were paid for it. We know the hangman was given a large sum of money and they probably asked one of the men from the city to do the job. Of course they put a black cloth over the hangman's head, so he might have slipped in for an hour, got paid, then returned to the city."

"And what did they do with the bell they found in Grandpa's pocket?" he asked, finally exhausting his questions.

"They say they gave it to the hangman himself, who slipped it into his pocket before making himself scarce. I suppose he wanted it as a memento or something. Sick, if you ask me. I of course didn't attend. I couldn't bear it. I stayed at home for three days before I was able to come out again. It was a most terrible time, Davey, two loved ones in the course of a few days."

Davey finished his milk and went over on his hands and knees to comfort Gran. They could hear 'Auld Lang Syne' being sung in 'The Wild Boar' and they both looked at the clock in amazement as it struck twelve, then resume its solitary ticking in the now otherwise silent cottage. Davey planted a kiss on Gran's warm cheek.

"I love you, Gran," he whispered in her ear. "Thank you for telling me. I'm so sorry you've had such a hard time."

"Don't you worry now, Davey," she responded. It was all a very long time ago. Of course I still miss them, but life goes on. So, you see, my boy, a grudge leads only to misery, as I told you."

"I'm going to tell Selwyn that we should either be friends or just leave each other alone!" Davey said defiantly.

"That's my boy, Davey, that's my boy!" Gran said with great pride.

Davey took out his diary and added, "This is going to be one for the diary, Gran. Don't worry, nobody will ever find it. I seek out the best hiding places!"

"Very well, Davey. Now you go upstairs and make yourself comfy. I'll come up when I've cleared the things away and we'll have a nice cuddle together!" She realised that he might well be asleep by the time it took her to tidy the cottage, wash the crockery and lay the breakfast table for the morning, but she knew that the notion of feeling safe and secure in bed with Gran would please him.

"Thanks, Gran. Good night," he said, planting another kiss on the other cheek and with that he grabbed his diary and ran up the stairs.

He was tired and so he only wanted to jot down the main points of what he'd heard that night. He also wanted to write down what he'd learnt from Gran, about not bearing a grudge and moving forwards, even if someone had upset you that day.

When he finished his last note, he scanned the room for a safe hiding place for his diary. He went to Gran's old chest of drawers and slowly pulled on the metal handle. The oak drawer was a little stiff, but eventually jerked open. He put the diary at the back of the drawer and went to close it, when his hand knocked against a trinket. Supposing it to be some jewellery, he pulled it slowly from the drawer. A shiver went up his spine as he took the curious object between his fingers. Had he not pushed his fingers in the dome, the little bell would have rung loud enough for Gran to hear. He realised his mind was playing tricks and dismissed his thought and fear – until he saw scratched on the inside the initials 'A.W.'. As he was about to return the object, he noticed the long, dark shadow of Gran, who was standing behind him.

Image

Josie blinked herself out of a daydream and saw the young woman opposite staring at her. She immediately averted her eyes to avoid feeling awkward, but then fixed her gaze on the woman's mouth. That way she could comfortably assess the appearance of the onlooker without having to look directly at her. She felt a sense of disgust as she traced the cherry-red lipstick around the mouth of the woman who, like Josie, was also waiting for the lift to arrive. Clearly the woman had been in a hurry as Josie noticed a tiny patch she must have missed in applying the bright makeup to her lips. Then, without looking straight into the eyes of the woman, Josie surveyed the eye-liner which had run slightly on her way to the building in which they were both standing. It looked like the woman had been crying. Strangely, instead of feeling any sympathy for the woman, Josie only felt repugnance. 'What's it looking at?' she said to herself, and from then on resolved to refer to the onlooker simply as 'It'.

She saw It's straw-like hair forming a cupped shape around a plump face and overlarge neck. Flicking her eyes for a moment, Josie quickly noticed It's shiny face that had been smeared with cream to cover up some of the acne that had refused to leave since adolescence. Josie then gazed at the floor, partly as relief from the revolting sight that stood before her and partly to survey the lower half of It. Yes, the interview skirt had been bought in some cheap sale and made It look like a frumpy schoolgirl waiting in the corridor to be reprimanded by the Headmistress. And those shoes! Who wore shoes like that nowadays! Just because It was smaller than most others of her age, why on earth did she have the raised platform shoes worn at discos in the seventies? Poor It, a short, fat ugly specimen of a creature who was trying so hard to cover up all her inadequacies!

Josie heard the lift whirring as it reached her level. As she watched the door slide open and erase her reflection Josie stepped into the lift, trying to leave It on the ground floor where she first met her. But It insisted on being with her. Standing alone in the lift as it made its slow ascent to the eighth floor, she was grateful for the wooden panelling that prevented It from being seen, but then drew a breath as the door re-opened. Josie stepped out of the lift, following signs to the room where she was to have her interview.

She handed her card to the receptionist, a middle-aged lady with a kind face, then excused herself as the nauseous feeling inside her caused her stomach to churn like curdled milk. Walking quickly to the bathroom sink she took some tissues and mopped them across her brow, only to see It once again staring at her. If her own image repulsed her so much what must others think?

She returned to her seat in the reception area, clutching her compact case and, flipping the mirrored lid to give herself a final check, encountered It sneering at her. She snapped shut the lid and thrust the compact case back into her handbag, panicking at the thought of having to present herself to others in public and forcing them to look at the disgraceful figure standing in front of them.

As she looked at her watch she noticed the nail polish which was already peeling. Just as she was about to apply some more, she caught another sight of It standing in the corner of the reception, looking sickly pale behind a pot plant. This time she did stare into It's eyes. Then she ran her eyes up and down the scrawny figure, grimacing into the mirror behind the pot plant, and finally she just sighed, dropped her shoulders and started to cry, quietly, feigning a cold as she dabbed her eyes with the tissues she had taken from the bathroom.

Josie had not noticed the receptionist looking at her, but she must have seen the entire event because there she was, crouched next to Josie with some more tissues and a plastic cup of water. When Josie looked at the receptionist she saw a warm, smiling face with a confidence that Josie wished she had. She remembered babbling out some words to the receptionist, apologising, then trying to explain that she knew she was good at her job and that she really wasn't afraid of the interview, but the receptionist simply put her finger to Josie's lips, softly whispered "Shh…" in a motherly tone, then said something that changed Josie's life. As she tucked some loose strands of hair behind Josie's ear, she said in a firm but gentle tone, "You know, sweetie, if you want others to love you, you first have to learn to love yourself."

Josie looked at the kind face looking at hers. This stranger wasn't telling her to go on a health farm or "Starve yourself at all costs if you want to start being noticed!" as her parents had advised her; neither did she tell her to "Just do your own thing and who cares about anyone else!" as her friends had been hammering away for months. She was simply telling her to look after herself, to take care of her body and to treat herself the way she wanted others to treat her.

She did not remember replying to the receptionist, but she did remember wiping her eyes, nodding, and standing up as she smoothed down her wrinkled skirt. She also remembered looking at her reflection in the mirror behind the pot plant before knocking on the interview door, then, with a wink and a smile to the receptionist, walking in to the sound of "Ah, Miss Wright, it is so good to meet you at last!"

"Yes", Josie kept saying to herself, "It is so good, It is so good."

Billet-Doux

(November 5, 1944)

Dear Richard,

Julian here! So sorry to hear you're ill! It must be really lonely for you in the school infirmary! We can't come upstairs to see you because Matron says Mr Watson feels you still need lots of rest. You're so lucky to have a House Master like Mr Watson! He must be the nicest person on the staff. Who else would bring delicious hot chocolate to a patient in the infirmary! Not like our Master, Dr. Chambers! We don't like him one bit! We're all scared of him and we just don't trust him: do you know, he reads out our test results to the whole class before we get them back and he gives you his dirtiest look if you say anything other than the precise answer he wants! So unfair! He is probably the worst German teacher in the world! I mean, who needs to learn that language anyway! He always threatens to contact our homes if we fail a test — Jenkins even threatened to run away from school this week because he was frightened Chambers might send more letters home to his parents complaining of his marks. He's so mean! Every time we ask for help he just threatens to send us to the Head! If I were bigger I'd feel like punching him right on the nose! I don't like his wife, either! She makes you drink that ghastly milk every day and eat mouldy spinach on Wednesdays! Ugh!

Anyway, Chambers knows he's not liked, I'm sure of that! But he can make life easier for himself if he will only try to be a bit nicer, especially to me, and my best friend, eh? Why is it that teachers like him feel that just because they're older and bigger than us, and that they have a degree, that they can talk down to us and treat us like dirt? I tried to spy on him in the staff room today, but lost courage when I saw Mr Watson coming! He's such a brick, he probably only would have laughed, but I didn't want to upset him. I do hope I'm in his House next Term.

Well, I must be going. Oh, I received a little message from my little sister. So sweet! She's played the same game we used to play when we were kids, you know, counting the number of words in a passage to read a message. So funny! I think she has a crush on you and has written you a little 'billet-doux' so you can remember her! It's overleaf. Hope you like it, Rich.

Keep well and hope to see you real soon. We could do with some cheering up — this rotten war is getting us all down.

Julian

2	81	95	32	33	91	81	233	119
66	67	52	101	103	184	110	17	27
113	22	23	158	159	160	14	88	137
140	320	81	240	125	52	117	118	74
253	122	22	258	95	30	229	79	248
91	266	201	256	23	95	19	210	331
17	27	174	215	45	170	171	16	201
330	278	280	3					